Chapter One

Miss Butler led her class out of the museum and across the grass. "Here is Jupiter Two!" she said. The children stared at the huge red and white rocket.

JUPITER 2

It was resting on its side and much
longer than a bus.
Reva gasped. "Is it a real rocket?"
she asked.
"Yes," said Miss Butler.
"Has it ever been to space?" asked Bobby.

Zoom to the Moon

JENNY McLACHLAN

ILLUSTRATED BY ANDY ROWLAND

BLOOMSBURY EDUCATION
Bloomsbury Publishing Plc
50 Bedford Square, London, WC1B 3DP, UK

BLOOMSBURY, BLOOMSBURY EDUCATION and the Diana logo are
trademarks of Bloomsbury Publishing Plc

First published in Great Britain in 2018 by Bloomsbury Publishing Plc

A catalogue record for this book is available from the British Library

ISBN: PB: 978-1-4729-5565-4; ePDF: 978-1-4729-5564-7; ePub: 978-1-4729-5563-0

2 4 6 8 10 9 7 5 3 1

Printed and bound in China by Leo Paper Products, Heshan, Guangdong

All papers used by Bloomsbury Publishing Plc are natural, recyclable products from wood grown
in well managed forests. The manufacturing processes conform to the environmental regulations of
the country of origin.

To find out more about our authors and books visit www.bloomsbury.com
and sign up for our newsletters

Miss Butler shook her head. She told the children that some rockets are built, but never get used. "The museum have put Jupiter Two here so you can see what a rocket looks like," she said. "You can even explore inside."

5

Reva looked at her best friend Bobby. They both loved space and wanted to be astronauts. Reva's name even meant "star".

"Poor rocket," said Bobby. Reva nodded. Imagine being built to soar through space, but never leaving planet Earth!

Miss Butler told the children they had half an hour to play before getting back on the coach. The others ran to the adventure playground, but Bobby and Reva went straight to the rocket.

Chapter Two

Inside the rocket they found child-sized space suits and lots of buttons to press. They had great fun jumping about and pretending to be astronauts.

They even climbed into the padded seats and did up the seatbelts. All the other children were still at the playground. It felt like the rocket belonged to them.

"I wish we could take Jupiter Two into space," said Bobby, running his fingers over the control panel.

"We can," said Reva. "We just have to do the countdown."

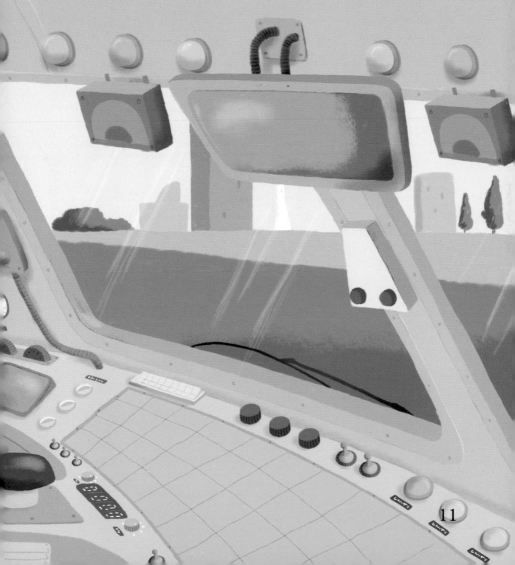

Together, they said, "Ten, nine, eight, seven, six, five, four, three, two, one!" "Lift off!" cried Bobby. But nothing happened. "Come on, Jupiter Two," said Reva, patting the rocket. "Don't you want to visit space?"

"We forgot to press the big button," said Bobby. He reached forwards and pushed down on the red button in the middle of the display panel.

There was a rumble and the rocket began to roar. The door shut with a clunk and the display panel burst into life. Buttons flashed and numbers zoomed round.

Slowly, the rocket tilted back until its nose was pointing up in the air. Bobby and Reva looked at each other in amazement. This was definitely the best thing at the museum!

Then Reva noticed that the roof of the museum was sliding past the window. "Bobby, I think we're moving!" she said. Soon they were passing through clouds. Then all they could see out of the window was bright blue sky.

Switches moved on the display panel and buttons pinged on and off. Bobby's heart beat fast with excitement. He wasn't scared because the rocket seemed to know exactly what it was doing.

"Is the rocket really moving or pretend moving?" Bobby said.

"I don't know," said Reva, with a grin. The rocket seemed as happy as Reva. A line of lights lit up on the display panel like a big smile.

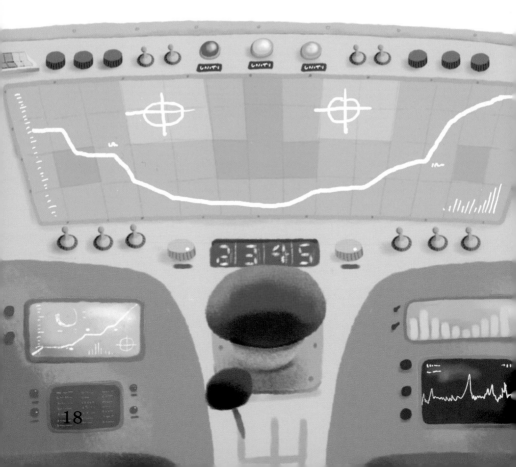

Chapter Three

The rocket soared higher and higher.
The blue sky vanished from the window.
Now Bobby and Reva were surrounded
by darkness and millions of stars.

The rocket stopped rumbling and shaking and Bobby's heart slowed down too.

"Are we in space?" he said, gazing at the stars.

"If we are in space then we'll be able to float," said Reva, then she took a deep breath and undid her seatbelt.

She drifted out of her seat and up into the air like a balloon. "Look at me!" she cried as she floated across the rocket and did a roly poly. "Come on, Bobby!"

Bobby undid his seatbelt and, just like Reva, he floated out of his seat. He did a roly poly too. In fact, he did five roly polies in a row until he felt dizzy!

"Wahoo!" he cried.
Soon Bobby and Reva were twisting
and turning and bouncing and bobbing
all over the rocket.

The rocket was having as much fun as them. Its lights flashed like a disco and alarms beeped and pinged.

Chapter Five

Bobby was just floating past the window when he saw something huge, and round and white.

"Look, Reva, it's the Moon!" he cried.

They pressed their faces against the window and watched as the Moon got closer and closer. It was lumpy and bumpy with craters.

Suddenly, the words "Moon Landing" flashed onto a screen. "I think we need to strap ourselves in," Reva said. They shot back across the rocket and landed in their seats.

The moment they did up their belts, the rocket began to shudder. Then it landed with a big bump.

Chapter Five

Bobby and Reva found two round helmets and pulled them on just as the door to the rocket hissed open.

With a loud "Whoop!" they jumped
out of the rocket and landed on the
surface of the Moon. Dust swirled
around them.

Reva took giant leaps and Bobby
followed in her footsteps.
Reva did a handstand and Bobby
bounced between craters.
While they played, the rocket watched
over them.

Just then, Reva noticed lights flashing
on the rocket. The door was starting to
close! She grabbed Bobby and together
they jumped back to the rocket.

They tumbled inside Jupiter Two just as the engines started. As they pulled off their helmets, moon dust floated around them.

"Oh no," said Reva, looking at the display panel. "We've only got five minutes until we need to be back on the coach!"

"Time to go," said Bobby. They rushed to their seats and did up their seatbelts. "But how do we go back?" asked Reva.

They looked at the hundreds of buttons and switches on the control panel. It was so confusing! But then the big red button started to glow. The rocket knew what they had to do.

Together, they reached for the button.
"Ready?" said Bobby
"Ready!" said Reva.
They pressed down on the button. The
rocket shook and roared. Slowly, it
lifted off the Moon.

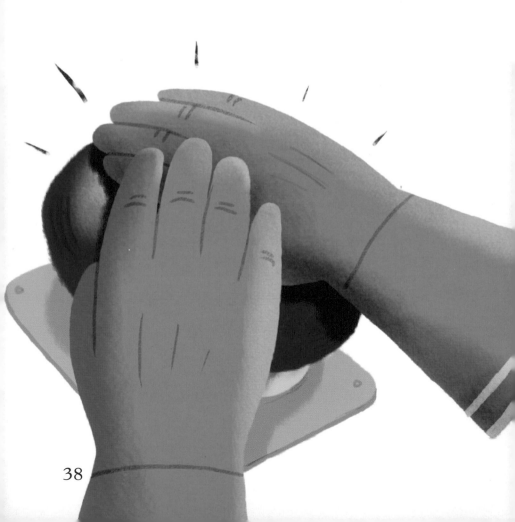

Then they were shooting back through space again, only this time they were heading home. Bobby and Reva could see Earth in the distance. It looked like a green and blue football that was covered in swirling clouds.

Jupiter Two moved closer and closer to their planet. Then the words "Earth Landing" flashed up on the screen. As the rocket's engines roared, Reva grabbed the hand rests and Bobby squeezed his eyes shut.

Jupiter Two landed with a thump, then the engines turned off and the rocket was still.

JUPITER 2

Bobby opened his eyes. The buttons had stopped beeping and flashing. Inside the rocket, everything was quiet. Outside, children were laughing and playing. The door hissed open.

Chapter Six

Bobby and Reva undid their seatbelts and slipped out of the padded seats. They walked across the rocket with wobbly legs. They hung their spacesuits back on the pegs, then went to the door and blinked into the sunlight.

Their friends were still in the playground. Miss Butler was sitting on a bench and drinking a cup of tea. "Hello, you two," she said. "What have you been up to?"

Reva and Bobby looked at each other
and grinned. "Exploring," said Reva.
"We went to the Moon!" added Bobby.
"That sounds like fun," said Miss Butler.
"I went to the café."

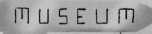

MUSEUM

Reva and Bobby sat next to each other on the coach. As they left the museum, they looked out of the window to say one last goodbye to Jupiter Two. The nose of the rocket seemed higher now, like it was pointing proudly towards space.

"Do you think we imagined going to
the Moon?" said Bobby. He knew it was
impossible to go to the Moon and back
in half an hour.

Before Reva could reply, she sneezed.
Grey dust swirled out of her hair. It fell
all over her arms and legs.

"Look," she said, sprinkling some of the dust into Bobby's hand, "moon dust!"